ASTRID'S ADVENTURE

ASTRID'S ADVENTURE

Hawys Morgan

Marta Orse

Collins

Contents

ASTRID'S FAMILY TREE

Mum

Dad

twins

Astrid

Karl

Uncle

Aunt

Helga

Olaf

ASTRID'S JOURNEY

York

UNITED
KINGDOM

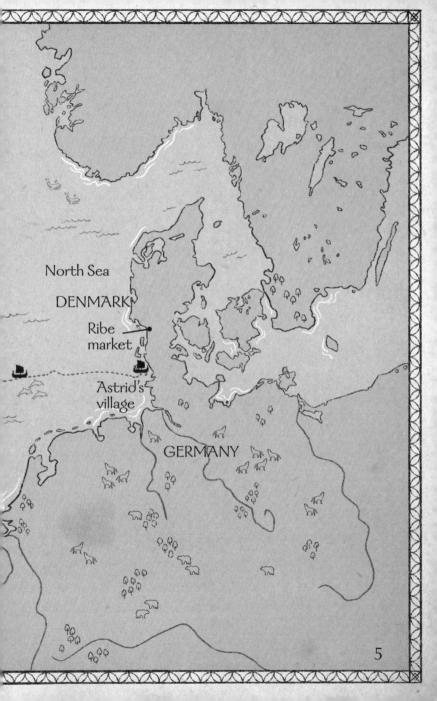

North Sea

DENMARK

Ribe market

Astrid's village

GERMANY

Chapter 1
Traveller's return

"Astrid! Astrid, are you listening to me?"

Astrid looked up at her mother who was standing in front of her with her hand on her hip. "Hmm?" she mumbled in reply.

"I was telling you that you're using the wrong colour wool! You should be using the yellow wool, not the red. You know the red wool is expensive and only for special cloth," scolded her mother.

Astrid looked down at the blanket she was weaving; her mother was right. "I'm sorry, Mum. I just can't concentrate. Dad and Karl should be back from their trip by now. I hope they are OK."

Her mother's expression softened. She bent down to give Astrid a hug. "I'm sure your dad and brother are fine. The wind changed direction this morning. It will help guide their ship over the sea, back home. No matter what scrapes your dad gets into during his trips, he always comes back to us safe and sound."

Astrid's dad travelled far and wide buying and selling things. He was with Astrid's uncle, and her twin brother Karl. They sailed across the oceans and then down the great rivers of Europe to the south, sometimes crossing land on foot.

They sold cloth, honey and wooden cups and plates. They would come home with beautiful silver jewellery, delicious spices and colourful glass.

Astrid's family shared a house with her uncle, her aunt, and her cousins Helga and Olaf. It was a crowded but happy home.

There was a loud croaking noise at the open door. "Jet!" said Astrid excitedly.

Jet was Astrid's pet raven. He looked at her with his intelligent, black eyes. Jet swooped in and out of the doorway, inviting Astrid to come outside. Astrid looked longingly at the bright blue sky beyond the door.

Her mother laughed and said, "OK, you can go outside. First, unravel the red wool. Then, why don't you go down to the beach? It's a lovely day. You can gather some seaweed and we'll dry it in the sun."

Astrid nodded enthusiastically. Dried, salty seaweed was one of her favourite snacks.

She quickly unravelled her wool, picked up a basket and ran happily out of the door.

She called out hello to her friends and neighbours as she made her way through the bustling village. Jet glided in the sky above her. Eventually, the narrow, busy streets gave way to vast green fields.

Astrid waved to her cousin Helga, who was weeding one of the fields.

Astrid's dad, uncle, brother and many other men from the village had been on their trading trip for six weeks. With so many men away at sea, all the village children had to help the women who remained at home.

Astrid shouted, "Weeding? Bad luck, Helga!"

Some jobs were better than others. Weeding made your back hurt.

The best job was probably fishing. Astrid and Helga loved sitting on the rocks with fishing lines, chatting and joking together. Sometimes, they went fishing in the bay with nets. Astrid had her own boat. She was a good sailor.

Astrid skipped down the path that led down to the beach. Salty air filled her lungs. She loved the sea. Somehow, she felt more alive when she was near it. She was fascinated by how it was always changing. Sometimes, it was a shimmering blue, the water lapping calmly at the sandy beach. Other times, grey waves lashed against the rocks and you could barely hear yourself think.

Astrid started collecting some of the slippery seaweed that grew along the shore. She paused for a moment to look out to sea. She thought about all the exciting places on the other side of the ocean. One day, she would explore the world, just like her twin brother Karl.

That was when she saw it. A tiny dot on the horizon. She screwed up her eyes. "Jet, can you see that?" she asked the bird who was hovering on the breeze just above her. "Could it be? Could it be Dad's ship?" The bird flapped his wings and flew part way out to sea before returning to Astrid, cawing loudly.

The dot was bigger now and Astrid could see the familiar shape of her dad's ship. She turned around and raced back towards the village. She ran as fast as her legs would carry her, all thoughts of collecting seaweed forgotten. She raced past Helga, who called out, "What's up, Astrid? What's the emergency?"

Astrid shouted her reply over her shoulder as she passed: "They're back! Dad's ship is back! Come on, Helga. Let's tell everyone!"

Together, they pushed their way through the village streets shouting, "They're home!"

Astrid's mother heard the commotion and joined the girls in the street. Her face showed a mix of excitement and fear.

Despite what her mum had said to Astrid earlier, sailing voyages were dangerous. You could never be sure everyone would make it home uninjured.

A crowd of villagers had gathered. They made their way down to the harbour to welcome the ship home. It was quite close now. Her mum had been right – the wind had helped them on the last stage of their journey.

Astrid and Helga stood hand in hand on the jetty. "Dad!" yelled Astrid, as his jolly face came into view. Helga hugged Astrid hard as she spotted her own dad.

Karl came to the edge of the ship and threw Astrid a rope, shouting, "Tie us up safely, Astrid!"

Astrid's mum sighed with relief as the crew jumped onto the jetty. She hugged her husband tightly and then called out to the crowd: "They're all home safe and sound. Let's have a feast to celebrate!"

The villagers clapped and laughed. Everyone loved feasts.

17

Chapter 2
A feast

Astrid wanted to help unload the ship. She couldn't wait to hear about the trip. However, there was a feast to prepare.

First, Astrid's aunt sent the girls off to collect goose eggs. They crept up to the nest quietly, hoping to go unnoticed, but the straw made Helga's nose tickle. She desperately tried to hold in the sneeze, but it was no good. A-TISH-OO! They just about managed to grab enough eggs before they were chased away by the snapping geese.

They dug up fresh carrots and collected berries and nuts. Jet followed them everywhere they went and snaffled the berries which were too high for the girls to reach.

Finally, Astrid and Helga picked up their fishing lines and settled on the rocks by the beach.

Astrid looked out at the waves and said, "One day, I'll go on an adventure."

Helga rolled her eyes and replied, "Yeah, right. They'll never let you, Astrid. Women and girls hardly ever get to go on trips. We're supposed to stay here and do the housework and farming."

Just then, Astrid's fishing line twitched. It was an eel! "Help me get it in the basket." The slippery eel was tricky to get a good hold of. It slipped out of Helga's hands and started to slither over the rocks. "We have to catch it! Eel is Karl's favourite!"

Astrid launched herself at the eel. She grabbed it with both hands. "Got it!" Then she lost her balance and toppled into a shallow pool. "Oops!" Both girls burst into laughter.

They put the eel safely in the basket and continued fishing. Before long, their basket was full of fish. It was time to head back.

The house was filled with smoke and the delicious smell of food cooking. Bread was baking on hot stones around the fire. Astrid's mum was stirring a big pot of goat stew.

Her aunt took the basket from them. "Well done, girls!" she said. "That's a great haul of fish."

Karl popped his head around the door carrying a small sack. "I brought you a present from our trip, Mum!"

"What is it?" she asked. She opened the sack – pepper! What a luxury. "Thank you, Karl! I'll grind some and add it to the stew."

She turned to Helga and Astrid. "Girls, go clean up, then put your best clothes on. We'll be celebrating soon!"

They ran down to the shore. Toddlers were splashing about in the water. Older children were swimming further out. Astrid and Helga waded in and started scrubbing the smell of fish off their hands.

Suddenly, there was a huge splash next to them. They were soaked to the skin!

Gasping in shock, Astrid shouted, "Which good-for-nothing did that ... KARL!"

Her twin popped up from under the water, grinning widely. "I thought you looked like you needed a proper wash!"

She tried to grab him so she could dunk him, but he slipped away laughing.

Helga giggled. "He's as slippery as the eels he loves to eat!"

With hair neatly combed and wearing smart, clean tunics, the girls greeted guests arriving at the feast. Gradually, the house filled with people, young and old. Everyone was wearing their best clothes and jewellery.

The crowd cheered as Astrid's dad and uncle arrived. Their trip had been a great success. They took their seats. Astrid and Helga brought them their special drinking horns. They only used them at special feasts and festivals. Then the cousins helped serve plates and bowls of stew, roast meats, vegetables and bread.

Chatter and laughter filled the air as families and friends shared their news from the past few weeks.

Once all the guests were served, Astrid filled her own plate. After several helpings of stew and a big chunk of bread and cheese, she leant back on the bench and sighed happily. The fire blazed in the middle of the room.

It was wonderful to see her father sitting next to her mother once more. She called over to him, "Dad! Tell us a story from your travels! Please!"

Her dad loved telling stories about his adventures. "OK, OK! If you insist!"

Astrid sat down on the bench next to him – she didn't want to miss a single word.

He started telling his tale ...

'A soft wind blew and led us south across the ocean. One night, Karl was keeping lookout while the rest of the crew slept. We awoke to hear him shouting, "Rocks! Rocks ahead!" How could that be? There hadn't been any rocks in this area on our previous trips. In the gloom, we saw a huge, grey, solid shape. Desperately, we tried to change the direction of the ship so we wouldn't crash into it.'

'Then my brother said, "Hang on! Those rocks are moving." At that moment, a great spurt of water erupted from the rock. It wasn't a rock, it was a whale! It was Karl's first trip. He wasn't to know we always see whales in that part of the ocean in late summer.'

Everyone laughed and called out, "More! Tell us more!"

Astrid's dad continued: 'The whale slipped silently beneath the water and we didn't see it again. You never know what is lurking down there. They say there is a giant monster with many legs called the kraken. It can destroy a ship with one blow. I hope we never meet it.'

'After we'd crossed the ocean, we sailed down wide rivers. We travelled day and night. Wolves howled at the moon. Mountains towered over us like sleeping giants. We made our way east where we found great buildings with many towers and onion-shaped domes.'

Astrid was entranced by his tales. She longed to see these sights.

BAKING VIKING BREAD

Most Viking bread was flat bread. The dough was shaped like a pancake and usually cooked on a fire in a frying pan. Sometimes, the bread was used as a plate. Sauces from the food soaked into the bread and the bread was eaten last.

Get a grown-up to help you if you want to try this!

AUNT INGRID'S FRYING PAN BREAD

INGREDIENTS:

- barley or oats
- water
- salt

METHOD:

Grind the barley or oats to make flour.

Knead the flour and water until it turns into dough.
Mix the salt into the dough.

Roll the dough into small balls.
Press down on each ball to
make a small flat pancake.

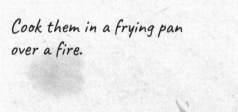

Cook them in a frying pan
over a fire.

31

Chapter 3
Dreams of faraway lands

Astrid woke up late after a long evening of singing and dancing. She quickly did her morning chores, then she went to find her father. He was busy unloading the ship. There were barrels and wooden boxes piled up everywhere.

"What did you bring back, Dad?" she asked.

Her dad cracked open a box. It was filled with rolls of colourful fabric. "Touch it," he said.

Astrid gently stroked the fabric; it was smooth and cool.

He explained, "It's called silk. It's the finest fabric in the world. They make it in the east."

It was nothing like the fluffy, itchy, sheep wool that Astrid spun and wove into cloth.

Astrid said, "The sheep in the east must look very different to our sheep to make fabric this smooth."

Her dad laughed. "It's not made from sheep's wool! Caterpillars called silkworms make it. They only eat mulberry plant leaves. Then, the caterpillar spins silk to make a cocoon around itself. The silkworm stays in the cocoon until it becomes a silk moth. People collect the cocoons and use them to make this fabric. They must collect thousands of cocoons to make enough silk thread to weave a small piece of fabric."

"Wow!" replied Astrid. "I can't believe something so beautiful comes from a bug!"

Her dad carefully resealed the box.
"It's very precious."

Astrid spent a happy morning with her father,
exploring the many different things he had
brought home. Jet was curious too. He hopped
about, peering into the boxes.

There were glittering jewels of every colour.
There were finely decorated silver cups and plates.
There were sacks full of spices that filled the air with
new and delicious smells.

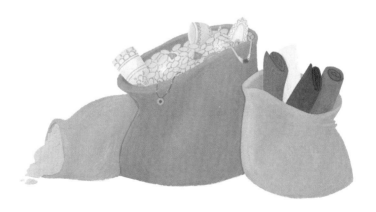

But for Astrid, the best thing of all were the stories her dad told as he opened each box.

He described strange animals with humps on their backs that could survive in hot, sandy deserts. He recounted seeing huge beasts with large, grey flapping ears and long tube-like snouts.

Astrid imagined herself alongside her father in these far-flung lands. How wonderful it would be!

Over the following weeks, Astrid helped the men mend the ship. She made ropes, nailed loose planks back into place and sewed up rips in the sail. She preferred working on the ship to housework or farming.

As they worked, the men talked about their adventures and the places they had seen.

They talked about shining marble palaces with colourful stained-glass windows. Her dad explained how craftsmen turned floors into wonderful pictures called mosaics by arranging little tiles of coloured stone.

Astrid listened and dreamed of going with them on their next adventure. It all sounded magical.

She loved her village, her friends and her family, but there was a whole world out there to explore.

One bright morning, Astrid was sitting outside the house enjoying the sunshine. She stroked Jet's head gently and said to the bird, "Today's the day, Jet. I'm going to ask Dad."

She walked down to the storeroom where her father was working. She took a deep breath and said, "Dad ... next time you go on a trip ... um ... do you think I could come with you?"

She shifted nervously from foot to foot, waiting for his reply. Astrid half expected her dad to argue with her, but it was worse than that. He *laughed.*

He patted her on the shoulder and said, "Don't be silly, Astrid! Women and girls don't go on trading trips. Your place is here, at home in the village."

For days, Astrid begged her father to change his mind, but he wouldn't listen.

At dinner one evening, she tried one last time. She pleaded, "Please let me come. You've seen over the past few weeks how helpful I can be. I can sail, I can mend the ship, I can prepare meals, I can build things. Mum, *you* know I'm ready!"

"She does have a point," said Astrid's mum. "And remember, I used to come on journeys with you when we first married."

"That was different. Astrid isn't old enough," her dad replied. He fished in his pocket and brought out a toy boat. "I know you love boats, so I got this for you, Astrid."

A toy boat?! Astrid couldn't believe it. To her father, Astrid was still a little girl. Why couldn't he see that she was ready to explore the world? He was never going to understand.

It wasn't fair that Karl went on all of the adventures, and she was stuck at home weeding and baking bread. They were the same age and she was just as brave and skilled as her twin brother!

The next morning, Astrid and Helga went down to the rocks to fish. Astrid was lost deep in her thoughts. Helga asked, "You're very quiet. Are you OK?"

Astrid replied, "I know Dad just wants to protect me, but it's not fair. Why can't girls be traders, too? I'm one of the best sailors in this village.

"I know you're happy here and I respect that. But it's not enough for me. I'm ready for this. If only Dad would let me prove it to him," Astrid explained. Jet edged closer to Astrid. "I want to be free to come and go, just like Jet," she said. Her face grew determined. "If Dad won't let me go on his trip, then I'll have to go by myself."

Helga knew that once Astrid had made up her mind, she was never going to change it. She also knew her cousin was clever and brave. "The sea is dangerous. I'm not going to come with you, Astrid. I'll miss you and worry about you. But I'll help you prepare in any way I can."

Chapter 4
Secret plans

Astrid started planning her adventure that
very afternoon. After she and Helga had completed
their chores, they went to look at Astrid's sailing boat.

"We must make sure it's watertight. Fill every gap,
check every nail," said Helga. They unfurled the sail
and checked it thoroughly for any rips or tears.

Astrid sailed the boat around the bay. It flew
lightly over the waves. She tested the oars, which
moved smoothly with a click-clack, dipping in and
out of the water as they pushed the boat forward.

Astrid rowed back to shore, then pulled
the boat onto the sand.

It was perfect. Astrid patted it happily and said,
"It may be small, but this boat can carry me safely
wherever I want to go!"

Helga said, "The men leave on their next trip in
two weeks. If you want to follow them, you need
to be ready by then."

Astrid's plan was to secretly follow her dad's ship.
Once they arrived at their first stop on their trip,
Astrid would reveal herself. There was no way her
dad and uncle would send her home alone in
her boat. They would have to take her with them
on their journey.

Astrid and Helga secretly collected supplies. Astrid needed food that wouldn't go bad on a long journey. They dried seaweed and smoked fish for the men's trip and prepared a little extra for Astrid's secret trip.

Astrid made herself a cosy leather sleeping bag to sleep in.

Helga was much better at weaving cloth than Astrid. She made several warm blankets and a thick cloak for her cousin.

Astrid kept it all in a little cave hidden in the cliffs that used to be their secret den when they were younger. She wove a strong rope and used it to pull her supplies into the cave, storing them away from prying grown-up eyes.

Gradually, the cave filled with neatly organised boxes and sacks.

47

They did all of this on top of their normal household tasks, but neither girl complained. It was essential that Astrid was well-prepared. They were exhausted in the evening, but proud of their efforts.

At dinner, both girls yawned widely at the same time.

"Why are you two so tired at the moment?" asked Astrid's mum.

"Uncle's snoring is keeping us awake," joked Helga.

Astrid's mum laughed. "You and me both! He snores like a giant napping after a midsummer feast."

"Hey!" protested Astrid's dad. "I don't snore! It's the goats snoring!"

Astrid laughed along too but, in reality, she hated deceiving her family. She wished there was another way – if only her father would change his mind and let her come with him. But he would never stop seeing her as his little girl. The only way her father would allow her to explore the world was by proving she was skilled enough, strong enough and brave enough.

Soon, it would be time to leave. Astrid counted down the days. Not long now. The ship would leave on Wednesday.

Crates and barrels of goods made by the villagers were packed and sealed. There were clay pots and warm wool blankets. There were combs made from deer antlers, carved with beautiful patterns. Barrels were filled with sweet honey from the village beehives. The storeroom was full to bursting.

Astrid, Helga and the rest of the family prepared food and clothing for the travellers. They filled barrels with fresh water for the sailors to drink on their journey. The men checked and double-checked the ropes, sails and anchors.

Finally, the day arrived. The ship was packed and the men were ready to leave.

Astrid's mum hugged her dad and asked, "Are you sure you should be going now? It's late summer. The autumn storms are just around the corner."

He gestured to the bright blue sky and replied, "The sun is shining, the breeze is light. The weather is perfect." Then he turned to Astrid and hugged her. "Be good. Help your mother. You're turning into a fine young woman, Astrid. One day, you will run your own farm!"

Astrid's shoulders sagged. She wanted to be an explorer, not a farmer!

She waved goodbye with her mother, her aunt, her cousins and their friends. The ship glided off over the water, heading east.

As soon as the ship had turned out of the harbour, Astrid and Helga raced down to the cliffs with Jet following. They fetched Astrid's supplies from the secret cave, packed them into the boat and pulled it to the water's edge.

Helga took Astrid by the shoulders and looked her in the eyes. "Are you sure you want to do this?"

Fear mixed with excitement made Astrid feel a little queasy. She took a deep breath. She needed to be calm. She had to do this properly.

She was determined. She said, "Tell Mum where I've gone. I don't want her to worry about me. But wait until this evening, otherwise she might send someone after me. I want to get a head start."

Astrid hugged Helga tightly. "Thank you, Helga." Then she pushed her boat into the water and leapt into it. Jet settled on the mast of her boat. She took the oars and started to row out to sea.

Helga called, "Good luck, Astrid! Bring me back some treasure!" and both girls smiled fondly at each other.

The little boat moved out into the bay. Astrid lifted the sail; it caught the breeze and the boat skimmed across the surface.

She couldn't see her father's ship, but she knew which way it had gone. She had listened carefully to her dad, uncle and Karl as they planned their journey. She knew which landmarks to look out for.

ASTRID'S DAD'S TRADING SHIP

mast

yard arm

sail

steering oar

prow

hull

oars

55

Chapter 5
At sea

Astrid didn't look back. She followed the cliffs to her right and the boat moved around the coast. The salty wind blew her hair off her face and she smiled happily. "I've done it, Jet!" she said to her bird. "We're having an adventure!" The sun shone down on her and the breeze carried them easily over the sea.

In the far distance, she could just make out her father's ship. It was important she kept her distance, so they didn't spot her, but she was reassured to see it up ahead.

Sea birds called out noisily overhead, diving into the water after fish. Big jellyfish with star-shaped patterns and long, dark tentacles floated gently past.

She sailed all day. As the sun started to set, dolphins leapt from the waves, chasing her boat. The world felt like a wonderful place.

Astrid scanned the shore for somewhere to stop. She didn't want to be at sea at night if she could help it. She spotted a small beach and brought her boat in. She made a little fire to keep her warm. She chewed on some dried fish and drank some water.

Then she snuggled into her sleeping bag. The stars shone brightly above her. Jet settled on a piece of driftwood and put his head under his wing. Astrid had never been alone before in her whole life. She was grateful to have Jet with her.

The next morning, Astrid set off once more. After an hour, she noticed a large rock that looked like a howling wolf. The nose of the wolf pointed out to sea. She knew that she had to turn when she reached this rock.

She said to Jet, "This is where it gets serious. Once I leave the coast behind, I'll only have the sun and the stars to guide me. I'll be in open sea."

Astrid's mother would know what she had done by now and would be worried. Astrid felt guilty, but she pushed these thoughts to the back of her mind. She needed to look forwards.

She turned the boat, and with her back to her homeland, Astrid sailed away from safety and into adventure ...

Astrid watched the position of the sun carefully to make sure she was sailing east. Concentrating was hard work, but she had to make sure she was going in the right direction. After a few hours, she couldn't see land at all. She would feel a lot happier if she could catch sight of her father's ship.

In the afternoon, clouds started to gather in the sky and the wind picked up. She looked at the grey sky with concern. The clouds now blotted out the sun. Panic rose in her chest – how would she find her way without the sun? Drops of heavy rain began to fall.

"Concentrate!" Astrid said to herself. "Just keep going in the same direction."

The wind grew stronger and the waves grew bigger. They pushed the little boat here and there as if it were made from paper. Astrid pulled her cloak up around her face. She and Jet hunkered down against the weather as the rain lashed them. Waves splashed into the boat, and it started to fill the bottom. After a while, it was almost up to Astrid's ankles.

She steered her way over the stormy waves. With the other hand, she bailed out the water for what felt like hours.

She was cold and her arms ached. Part of her longed to be back home, next to the warm fire with her family around her.

She was relieved when the winds eventually dropped and the sky cleared. According to the sun, Astrid was still heading east, but had the storm blown her off course? With no land in sight, it was impossible to say.

Just then, a great grey creature silently rose from the water. It was the size of an island! A spray of water erupted from its blowhole. Her boat rocked and she grabbed the sides, worried the boat might flip over. The boat steadied itself. Astrid sat as still as she could – she didn't want to scare it, whatever it was.

Then she realised that it must be a whale. A smaller whale emerged next to it – a mother and her baby. Astrid gazed at the magnificent animals.

A minute later, they dipped under the surface and were gone. Then she remembered something from one of Dad's stories – they always saw whales feeding on their late-summer trips. She must be going the right way!

That night, Astrid didn't sleep. She watched the stars twinkling in the sky, using them to find her way. Jet kept lookout, flying ahead.

Around mid-morning, he squawked excitedly. It was her dad's ship in the distance! And even better, Astrid could make out land on the horizon. Now, her aim was to catch up with her father and explain everything. They were too far from home to send her back now.

Gradually, she got closer to her father's ship, but not before night arrived. They would be reunited tomorrow!

In the early morning, a sea fog crept across the flat surface of the ocean. Astrid was surrounded by a wall of grey. How would she ever find her dad's ship? The mist soaked her hair and clothes.

Seagulls squawked eerily somewhere above, but it was impossible to tell where the birds were. They fell silent and everything was quiet, except for the gentle lapping of the waves against the boat.

Astrid shivered. What might be lurking out there in the fog? Sea serpents that could break her boat in two with one strike? Maybe a mighty kraken, with long, octopus tentacles that could pluck her from her seat?

Chapter 6
Fog

Astrid jumped as something fluttered near her face, imagining all kinds of monsters. She breathed a sigh of relief when Jet landed on her shoulder. His clever, black eyes gave her courage. She rowed forwards slowly. Every so often, she stopped to listen.

She heard the seagulls again. Large groups of seagulls usually stayed close to shore. She might be near land.

CRASH! She heard a splintering of wood and men shouting. Where was it coming from? How far away? It was so hard to tell with the fog! It could be her father's ship. She had to help them!

Jet croaked and took off quickly into the fog.

Astrid sat alone for what felt like a lifetime. She could hear dull shouts from somewhere out there. She scanned the fog surrounding her, looking for Jet or her father's ship.

Finally, Jet returned. He cawed loudly and flew back and forth.

"Do you want me to follow you, Jet?" asked Astrid. He cawed again, loudly. Astrid started rowing once more, following Jet. His feathers glistened with little drops of water, making him look like a shining black star against the sickly, grey fog.

Now black rocks were emerging around her. Wide-eyed seals lay on some of the rocks, gazing at her in surprise.

Her little boat was nimble enough to safely move around the rocks. The shouting was getting louder. Jet led her onwards, closer and closer.

And then suddenly, the ship reared up in front of her. She could see that it was caught on the rocks. The wood creaked as the ship moved backwards and forwards with the waves.

"Please, please, let everyone be OK!" she repeated to herself. Thankfully, she couldn't see any holes in the hull, although some of the wooden planks were a bit bashed and cracked.

She rowed around the outside of the ship, while Jet flew up to the deck. She heard her father's confused voice say, "It can't be ... Jet? Is that you?"

Astrid shouted up, "Dad! I'm down here!"

She saw her father peer over the edge of the ship. "Astrid? What on earth are you doing here?!"

Astrid replied, "Never mind that for now. Is anyone hurt?"

"Your brother is hurt. Karl fell when we hit the rocks. I think he's broken his arm," said her dad.

"I'll get him to shore where we can try to help him," said Astrid.

Her dad tied a rope around Karl's waist and the other end to the ship itself.

He gently lowered Karl into Astrid's boat, before climbing down himself. He gave Astrid a huge bear hug. Then they rowed to the shore.

On the beach, Karl said, "I'll be OK. You must get everything off the ship in case it gets damaged."

Astrid and her dad went back and forth transporting boxes, barrels and men to dry land.

Finally, Astrid flopped onto the sand next to Karl. She was exhausted. Karl looked pale. His right arm hung limply by his side. Although Astrid was tired, she had to help her brother.

She gently rolled up his sleeve. She could see his arm was broken – it was at an awkward angle. She ripped some fabric into strips. She warned him, "I need to make your arm bone straight again. It's going to hurt."

Karl cried out in pain as Astrid straightened the bone. Then she made a sling for him.

"Thanks, Astrid," said Karl. "That feels much better." He had more colour in his cheeks now.

Astrid's dad and uncle sat down next to them. Her dad said crossly, "I can't believe you were so foolhardy to take to sea alone! What were you thinking?" But then he paused and his tone softened. "But ... I'm pleased you are here. You really saved the day."

Astrid explained how she had carefully planned her journey and followed his ship. "I want to explore the world, Dad. I'm ready. You wouldn't listen."

He hugged her and said, "I'm sorry, but it could have been so dangerous alone in that small boat of yours."

At that moment, the sun broke through the fog. Bright rays of sunlight warmed their tired bodies.

After they had rested a little, Astrid and her dad went out in her boat to examine the ship. Together, they patched it up.

"Thankfully, it's only minor damage," said her dad.

"Look, the tide is coming in," said Astrid. "I think the rising water will lift the ship off the rocks."

They climbed onboard, attaching Astrid's little boat to the ship with a rope. They guided the ship away from the rocks and anchored it safely in the bay.

They returned to shore. Astrid's uncle was looking at Karl with concern. "I don't think Karl should continue on this trip. He should return home and let his arm heal properly there."

Astrid knew what she had to do. "I can take Karl back in my boat. I know the way and I'm a good sailor."

Her dad smiled at her and said, "I know you are. I'm sorry I never saw it before. You've shown courage, strength and determination coming here and helping us like you did."

"Thanks, Dad," said Astrid, blushing with pride. She started to walk over to her boat. "I'll check the boat over before we go."

"Wait!" he said. "I think your uncle should take Karl back in your boat. They can let your mum know you're OK – she must be so worried! Why don't you come on the trip with me in the ship? There are so many adventures waiting for us out there."

Astrid couldn't believe her ears! She ran into her dad's open arms. "Thank you! I won't let you down. I promise."

BONUS

My travel journal by Astrid

We saw the Northern Lights.

We sold our goods at a market. By the end of the day, we had lots of silver coins.

Dad bought a gold arm ring for Mum at the market. She's going to love it!

A bear tried to steal our honey.
Dad scared it away by blowing his horn!

We met Dad's friend, Bilal.
He's a trader from the east.
He let me ride his camel!

Finally, we arrived in Constantinople. I can't wait
to tell everyone back home about my adventures!

BONUS

VIKING FREE TIME

TOYS

Children played with homemade wooden toys, like toy dolls, animals and model boats.

Grown-ups played a board game that is sometimes called "Viking chess".

MUSIC

Vikings loved singing and dancing. Some children played simple musical instruments, like pipes and whistles made from animal bone.

SPORT

In the summer, Vikings enjoyed swimming, running and wrestling.

In the winter, they would often ice skate on frozen rivers and lakes. The ice skates were made from animal bones.

81

DAYS OF THE WEEK

Most days of the week were named after Viking gods and goddesses.

Sunday was named after the sun goddess Sol – Sol's day.

Monday was named after the moon god Mani – Mani's day.

Tuesday was named after the god of war Tyr – Tyr's day.

Wednesday was named after
the most powerful god,
Odin, also known as
Woden – Woden's day.

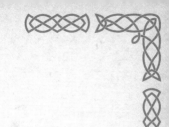

Thursday was named
after the god of thunder
Thor – Thor's day.

Friday was named
after the goddess of love
Frigg – Frigg's day.

Only **Saturday** is not named
after a Viking god or goddess!

MYTHICAL VIKING MONSTERS
SEA CREATURES

The kraken

The kraken was usually described as being like
a giant octopus or squid, big and strong enough to
destroy a whole ship or drag a sailor into the sea.

The field-back

This monster was a huge whale. It was so big that
some sailors mistook it for an island. As soon as
a sailor stood on its back, it would sink beneath
the surface of the ocean – taking the sailor with it!

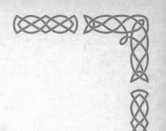

The sea serpent

This snake-like serpent lived under the oceans. It was so long that its body could coil around the whole Earth, and its movements under the sea caused dangerous storms.

LAND CREATURES

Fenrir

Fenrir was a giant wolf who was chained up by some Viking gods. Vikings feared the day he might break out of his chains. There were also giants and other strange creatures, such as an eight-legged horse!

About the author

Why did you want to be an author?

I've always loved reading. As a child
I had different reading spots around
my home. I would read in bed, in the bath,
in a hammock, in my treehouse. I adore
books, so what could be better than writing
them myself?

Hawys Morgan

How did you get into writing?

The first book I wrote was a non-fiction book about the many
animals and bugs that live in an oak tree. Since then I've written
over 50 reading books!

What is it like for you to write?

First, I do lots of research so I really understand the world I'm
going to write about. Next, I plan and then I write. I usually type
furiously for about 20 minutes and then I spend ages looking out
of the window! Finally, I reread and edit it.

**What book do you remember loving when you
were young?**

I had a wonderful history book that was divided into four sections:
Medieval knights, Ancient Romans, Ancient Egyptians and
… Vikings! It described everyday life and I found it fascinating.
I still have it and I must have read it hundreds of times.

Why this book?

There's more to Viking history than fierce raiders burning villages to the ground! I wanted to write about the Vikings who settled all over Europe and North America and who traded goods far and wide. I also wanted to put a girl at the centre of the story, as women and girls are often left out of books about Vikings.

How does this book relate to your own experiences?

When I was young, I used to go on long sailing trips across the Irish Sea with my family. I always looked for animals like seals, dolphins and jellyfish. So, Astrid's journey across the sea relates to that.

What do you hope readers will get out of the book?

Astrid didn't want the farming life her family had planned for her. Through hard work and determination, she changed her future. I hope readers will be inspired to follow their own paths in life, just like Astrid.

Why Vikings?

We often talk about the Vikings as if they were temporary visitors, but they never really went away. Viking words are part of our language. Cities like York were settled by the Vikings. Many people are descended from Vikings. I think we need to rediscover our links to the Vikings.

About the illustrator

A bit about me ...

Hi, I'm Marta and I'm an illustrator based in the south of Spain, near the sea. I have worked for publishers and magazines all over the world. I love spending time in nature, with animals, going to concerts, reading and making pottery.

Marta Orse

What made you want to be an illustrator?

I grew up in a house with many illustrated books and enjoyed reading them. That's how I realised how beautiful it is to be able to also narrate a story with images.

How did you get into illustration?

When I was studying fine art at university, I got my first commission as an illustrator. But it wasn't until a few years later that I realised how much I enjoyed illustrating that book and that I wanted that to be my profession.

What did you like best about illustrating this book?

I really enjoyed drawing this family of Vikings and learning about them but I especially loved drawing the scenes of Astrid with her little boat at sea.

What was the most difficult thing?

The most difficult thing for me to draw was the Hagia Sophia in Constantinople, because it is such a great building, and also Dad's Viking ship, as I had never drawn one before.

Is there anything in this book that relates to your own experiences?

Oh yes, I was the youngest in my family and my sister and older cousins could do things that I couldn't. I always wanted to go on adventures, travel and meet new people and cultures, which eventually led me to live in different cities all over the world.

How do you bring a character to life in an illustration?

I ask myself questions to find out more about their tastes, concerns, personality ... and so connect better with them.

Did you have to research the Vikings before illustrating the book?

Absolutely! I've read a lot about them before, and while drawing this book I was delighted to discover things I didn't know, like that they ate oatmeal.

Which of the characters was the most fun to draw? Why?

I really enjoyed drawing Astrid and Helga, and their beautiful relationship. Oh, and Jet the raven too!

Book chat

How would you describe Astrid?

Do you think Astrid changed between the start of the story and the end? If so, how?

Which scene in this book stands out most for you? Why?

If you had to pick one scene to act out, which would you choose? Why?

Do any characters in the book remind you of someone you know in real life? If so, how?

How do you think Astrid's mum felt when she realised Astrid was missing?